This is Reggie Mouse

He is quite daring.
Many would say that
he likes to cause
a bit of a commotion.

However, Reggie would
say he is only searching
for adventures!

Reggie Mouse and his friends
live in the amazing forest
of Bad Fusch, where there
is always something fun happening.

Let's follow Reggie Mouse
and his friends on their
latest adventure.

Reggie is sitting
on his favourite branch
with his friends
Malin, the Monkey,
and Sedric, the Marmot.

Suddenly, they hear a rumbling noise coming closer, getting louder and louder.

"What could that be?" asks Malin calmly while she eats nuts from the tree.

The three friends listen carefully to the sound when unexpectedly a red car appears.

Reggie, Malin and Sedric watch closely as two Yoomans get out of the car.

The Yoomans are pointing and making lots of noise.

"Blah blah blah"
is what it sounds like.

"I'm getting a better look," says Reggie.

"No! Wait!" Sedric says, but it is too late.

Reggie hops straight from the branch and scurries through the grass to get closer.

Reggie is crouching down only a short distance away. He notices the closer Yooman has spikey hair.
Reggie watches curiously for a moment.

He notices the Yooman further away has a big bushy beard.

Suddenly, the closer Yooman stops making noises and looks up in Reggie's direction.
"Oh no!" thinks Reggie, as he scurries back to his favourite branch in the tree.
"I think he saw me," he says to his friends.

Sedric, cautious as always, looks at Reggie and says, "Why would you do that, are you crazy?"

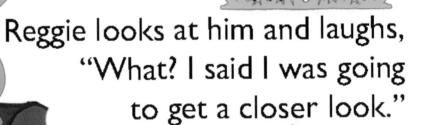

Reggie looks at him and laughs, "What? I said I was going to get a closer look."

Malin giggles and continues eating the tiny ants that she grabs off the tree.

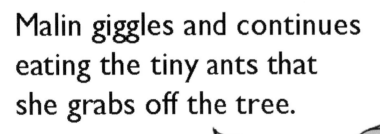

Sedric then asks Reggie, "Well, you got your closer look, who are they? Can you tell what they want?"

Reggie replies, "I can't tell. I have never seen those Yoomans before, I wonder what they are doing."

Reggie thinks long and hard.

"I bet Laura Frog has seen them before,
Laura Frog knows everything that goes on
in this forest," Malin says.

"You're right! Let's visit her at Frog Lake
to see if she can help us work it out,"
suggests Sedric.
"Yeah!" they all shout before heading off to
find Laura up at Frog Lake.

Even though this little lake is full of frogs happily hopping everywhere, they find Laura Frog instantly. She is the only one not moving at all as she is deep in her daily afternoon meditation.

Reggie scurries over to Laura and tickles her right on the top of her head with his tail.

Laura Frog opens her eyes to see her friends and says, "I could smell you all from two meters away! What mischief are you three up to today?"

"We saw a red car with two unfamiliar Yoomans, one with spikey hair and the other with a bushy beard. They were pointing and making noises and we are trying to get to the bottom of it. "Can you help?" asks Reggie excitedly.

"Let's all go and have a further look" says Laura.

Investigating together is their favourite thing to do,
so they know this is going to be yet another
great day. They begin their journey to figure out
the mysterious Yoomans.

"We all learn by asking!" Malin says as she eats a handful of red berries.

Finally, they spot the Yoomans who are now doing funny-looking stretches. The friends scurry, hop, and crawl beside a bush near the Yoomans to get the perfect view.
"Ahh, yoga at last!"
says Laura,

Malin the Monkey, Sedric the Marmot, Laura Frog and Reggie Mouse spend the rest of the afternoon following the Yoomans until it is time for their afternoon snack.

Instructed by Laura Frog, they practise yoga behind the bush in the magical calm of the forest of Bad Fusch.

Author notes, information, links and legal.

Special thanks to Catherine Jones for your valued input.

To keep up to date with all the latest information and future releases visit Facebook page www.facebook.com/reggiemouseandhisforestfriends Don't forget to like, share and leave a review; it inspires me to keep going.

Bad Fusch is a real place in the Alps of Austria. You can visit in the summer months and explore the forest, lakes, historic heart pool and kneippanlage. For information about the region visit www.bruck-fusch.at/badfusch

The Adventures of Reggie Mouse and his Forest Friends is written and illustrated by Jonnie Tash; published by John Swallow.

ISBN 978-3-9505006-0-8

Reggie and Friends will be returning for more forest adventures...

Printed in Great Britain
by Amazon